This book belongs to:

_____

_____

_____

For the Illustrati.
Power to the pencils!

HODDER CHILDREN'S BOOKS

First published in Great Britain in 2021
by Hodder and Stoughton

Text and illustrations copyright © Elys Dolan, 2021

HB ISBN: 978 1 444 94861 5
PB ISBN: 978 1 444 94862 2

1 3 5 7 9 10 8 6 4 2

Printed and bound in China.

FSC
www.fsc.org
MIX
Paper from
responsible sources
FSC® C104740

Hodder Children's Books
An imprint of Hachette Children's Group
Part of Hodder and Stoughton

Carmelite House, 50 Victoria Embankment, London, EC4Y 0DZ

An Hachette UK Company

www.hachette.co.uk
www.hachettechildrens.co.uk

WHAT ABOUT THE TOOTH FAIRY?

Elys Dolan

Hodder
Children's
Books

TOOTH
CHUTE

COMING,
TOOTHY!

This is the
TOOTH FAIRY.

Hi!

And this is her
assistant, Pérez the
TOOTH MOUSE.

FRAGILE: TEETH
IN TRANSIT

Hola!

The Tooth Fairy and Pérez have a VERY important job.

Every night, they pack up lots of coins and set off in search of teeth.

They check under pillows, collecting each tooth they find . . .

. . . and leaving a coin in return.

And at the end of the night, they take all the teeth home . . .

...to add to their

MASSIVE CASTLE!

(Yes, it is all made of teeth, but they don't mind that.)

Tooth tree

Cheese Plant

Tooth Fairy's toothbrush collection

World's largest toothbrush

Library Tower

Time for a good clean!

Tooth Fairy's room

Teeth roof

Teeth walls

Perez's room with cheese and hat collection

Shower Tower

Living room

Teeth toilet

Grand Hall

Spare teeth storage

Pérez's secret cheese

HMS MILK TOOTH

TOOTHY! I've lost my cheese!

I ♥ ♡

Life is pretty great for the Tooth Fairy. But lately there's been one thing bothering her . . . .

Everyone knows **FATHER CHRISTMAS** gets Christmas Day.

The **EASTER BUNNY** has Easter, of course.

Looking good, Chad!

Valentine's Day belongs to **CUPID** (who likes people to call him Chad).

And then there's Halloween, which is run by **JACK O'LANTERN** and his cronies.

"I think you should ask for your **OWN SPECIAL DAY!**" Pérez told the Tooth Fairy.

And that's exactly what she did. The next day, the Tooth Fairy signed up to compete in the

CELEBRATION CHALLENGE.

Children really like what I do, so I think I should have a day too. We can call it TOOTH DAY!

E. BUNNY

F. CHRISTMAS

Tooth Day? What a ridiculous idea!

SAMPLE

The Celebration Committee were sceptical, but Tooth Fairy was determined. **"JUST GIVE ME A CHANCE!"**

"OK, Tooth Fairy," said Father Christmas.
"If you want your own day, you're going
to have to **PASS OUR TESTS.**"

THE PEOPLE'S
REPUBLIC OF HALLOWEEN

So they set off to Christmas Town for
the Tooth Fairy's **FIRST** challenge.

CHRISTMAS TOWN

THE
EASTER
PLAINS

VALENTINE'S
BAY

THE
TOOTH
CASTLE

The North Pole

Father Christmas set the **FIRST TASK.**

For a day to be jolly, there must be BEAUTIFUL DECORATIONS of things we all love. Can you decorate a fabulous Christmas tree, Tooth Fairy?

"That's **NOT** jolly, or festive, or even vaguely merry," said
Father Christmas. "It's just . . . **WEIRD!** I'm afraid it's a **NO** from me."

It's easy!
I just push...

...and, OH!
There's an egg!

POP!

NOW YOU try.

Weird!

But however the Easter Bunny managed to make those eggs,
the Tooth Fairy could not do the same.

PUSH...

PARP!

How
embarrassing.

"Well that is **NOT** very Easter!" said the Easter Bunny. "It's a **NO**
from me. We'd better move on to the **VALENTINE'S TEST.**"

Chad's test was a bit of a surprise.

The best days are full of **LOVE!** And how do we make people fall in love? Shoot them with arrows, of course! But not the pointy ones – these are arrows of love.

This bow might be a bit big for me! Can I have some time to practise?

BOING!

MY HAIR!

OW!

"Nobody is feeling the love now!" said Chad. "It's a **BIG NO** from me. Get me some hair gel and let's go to the People's Republic of Halloween."

The Halloween test really was the **LAST** straw for the Tooth Fairy.

So she left.

Back at the Tooth Castle, the Tooth Fairy went to her bedroom and refused to come out. Pérez missed her a lot.

Toothy, come out! We can build a tooth tower? I have cheese!

No, Pérez, I'm NOT coming out. If I'm NOT good enough to have a day, then I'm NOT good enough to be the Tooth Fairy.

Pérez knew he wasn't the only one who would miss the Tooth Fairy. The children would still expect their teeth to be collected! So, he put on his angry hat and went to speak to the Celebration Committee.

That night, the Celebration Committee set out to collect the teeth.
But it wasn't the easy job they were expecting . . .

They realised they needed the Tooth Fairy back.

Back in her room, the Tooth Fairy
heard a knock at the door.

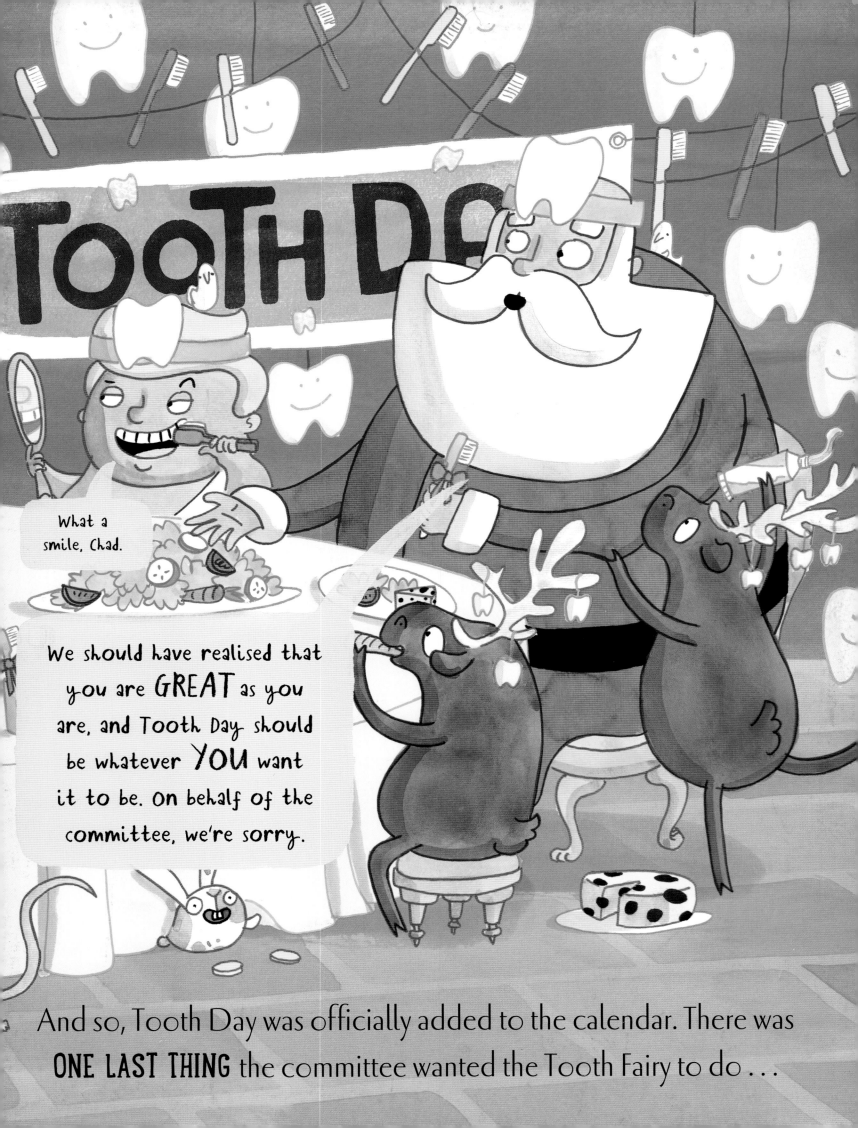

And so, Tooth Day was officially added to the calendar. There was **ONE LAST THING** the committee wanted the Tooth Fairy to do . . .

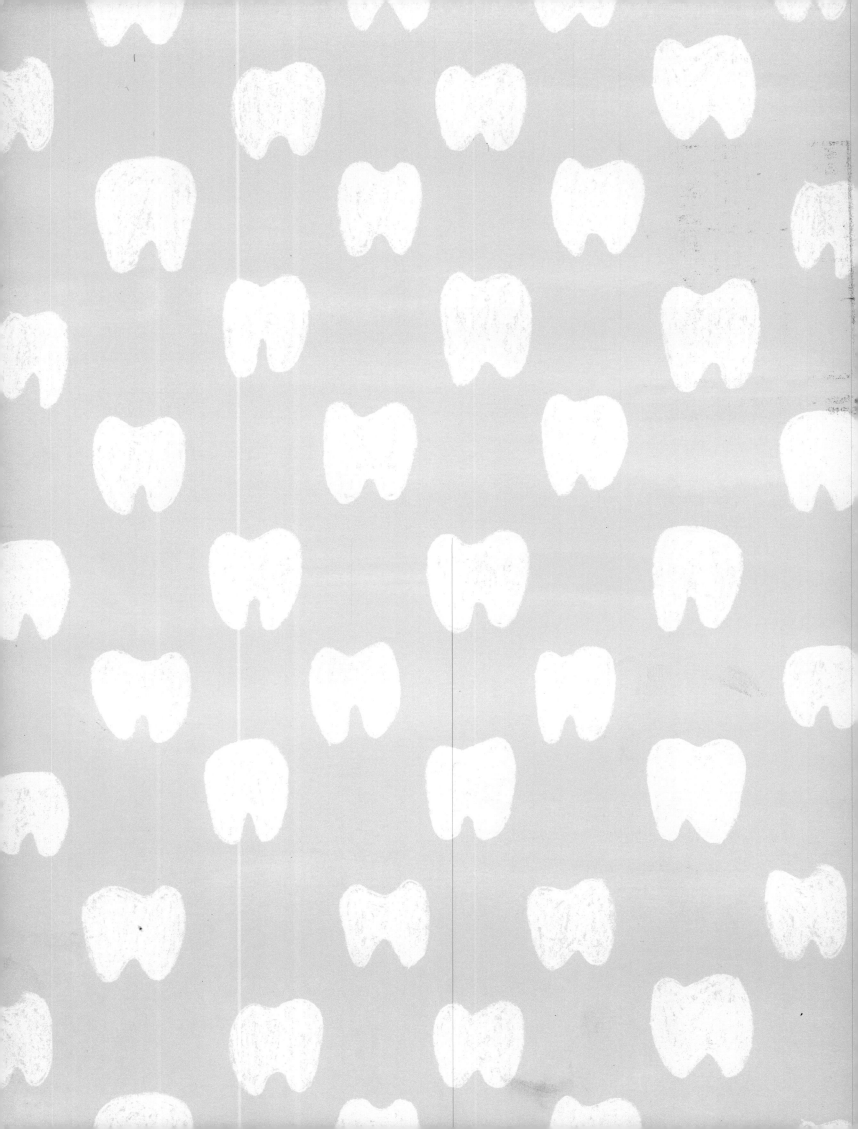